KT-559-369

000003066061

**DUDLEY
LIBRARIES**

000003066061	
Askews & Holts	14-Dec-2020
JF SR	£5.99
2CR	

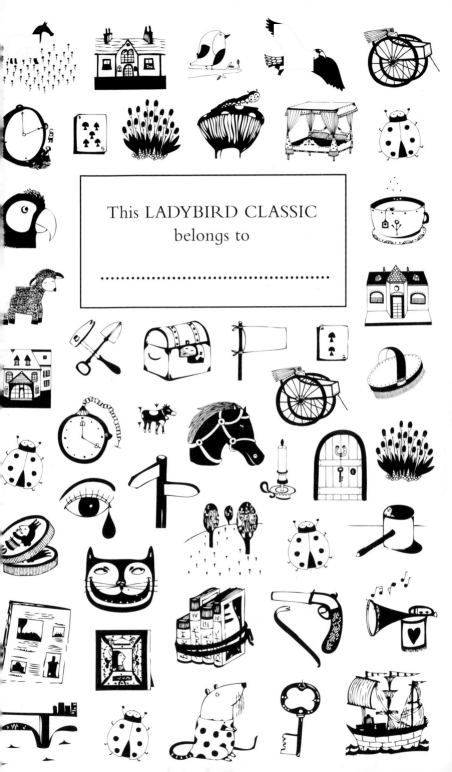

This LADYBIRD CLASSIC
belongs to

....

A History of the Author

Charles Dickens was born in 1812.
When he was twelve years old, his father,
a clerk, was imprisoned for debt and
Charles was forced to work in a warehouse.
These experiences affected him deeply,
and many of the stories and books he later
wrote are concerned with the hardships
suffered by the poor in Victorian England.

Chapter illustrations by Valeria Valenza

A catalogue record for this book is available from the British Library

Published by Ladybird Books Ltd
80 Strand London WC2R 0RL
A Penguin Company

008

© Ladybird Books Ltd MMXII

LADYBIRD and the device of a Ladybird are trademarks of Ladybird Books Ltd

All rights reserved. No part of this publication may be reproduced,
stored in a retrieval system, or transmitted in any form or by any means,
electronic, mechanical, photocopying, recording or otherwise,
without the prior consent of the copyright owner.

ISBN: 978-1-40931-125-6

Printed in China

LADYBIRD 🐞 CLASSICS

Oliver Twist

by Charles Dickens

Retold by Brenda Ralph Lewis and Ronne Randall
Illustrated by Steve Horrocks

Contents

CHAPTER ONE

Oliver's Early Life

IN THE FIRST half of the nineteenth century, there existed in most English towns a grim building known as the workhouse. This was where the parish authorities sent the aged, the homeless and the poor who could not work and had nowhere else to go.

It was in the workhouse that Oliver Twist was born. Oliver's mother, a beautiful young woman, had been found lying in the street the night before. No one knew who she was, and she died within minutes of giving birth. Oliver Twist was given his unusual name by Mr Bumble, the parish official in charge of the workhouse.

At the age of ten months, Oliver was sent out to a branch-workhouse, to be brought up by the elderly Mrs Mann. She looked after twenty or thirty poor orphans for a small weekly fee paid by the parish. Mrs Mann used most of this money for herself, and very little to feed and clothe the children. Consequently, Oliver, like all his comrades, grew into a small, pale, thin child.

When Oliver was nine, Mr Bumble came to bring him back to the workhouse so that he could be taught a trade with other boys his age.

As miserable as Oliver had been

whilst at Mrs Mann's, he was even more unhappy at the workhouse. He missed the friends he had grown up with, and he was hungrier than he had ever been. All the boys were ever fed was gruel.

One evening, Oliver thought he would go mad with hunger. He had finished his allotted bowl of gruel and still felt a raging emptiness inside him. Desperately, with his bowl and spoon in hand, he approached the master of the workhouse.

'Please, sir,' said Oliver, 'I want some more.'

The master was stupefied. No one had ever dared to ask for more. 'What?' he roared.

'Please, sir,' Oliver repeated quietly, 'I want some more.'

Enraged, the master struck Oliver on the head and locked him up in a dank and dismal cell. He remained there for weeks.

Rescue from this wretched existence came in the form of Mr Sowerberry, an undertaker who took Oliver as an apprentice.

At the Sowerberrys', Oliver was fed table scraps and had to sleep among the coffins. Still, he didn't complain.

But one day he got into a fight with Mr Sowerberry's surly assistant. Mr Sowerberry was so angry that he threatened to send Oliver back to the workhouse.

Oliver was terrified. He couldn't bear the thought of returning to the workhouse. So he decided to run away.

CHAPTER TWO

Oliver Comes to London

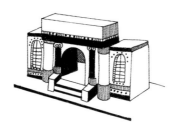

OLIVER TWIST SAT wearily on a doorstep and shivered. The sun was just rising over the town, and the chill of the night was still in the empty streets.

Oliver was too exhausted to move. He had walked seventy long, hard miles since running away from Mr Sowerberry, and his feet were sore and bleeding. He ached all over, and he was weak with hunger.

But he did not regret running away – even this was better than the workhouse.

An hour or two passed, and people began appearing in the streets. They saw the ragged and weary orphan sitting on the doorstep, but most of them looked away and hurried on.

Then, all of a sudden, Oliver felt that someone was staring hard at him.
He glanced up and saw a snub-nosed, rough-looking boy standing close by, looking him up and down with sharp, ugly little eyes.

'Hello!' the boy greeted Oliver chirpily. 'What are you doing here?'

'I'm hungry and tired. I've been walking for seven days,' Oliver replied in a weak voice.

The boy whistled in wonderment. 'Seven days!' he exclaimed. Then, unexpectedly, he gave Oliver a kind look. 'You'll be wanting grub. Don't worry, I'll pay!'

The boy was as good as his word. When Oliver had wolfed down the first real meal he had had for days, the boy asked: 'Going to London?'

'Yes,' Oliver told him.

'Got any lodgings?'

'No,' said Oliver ruefully.

'I suppose you want somewhere to sleep tonight, then?' said the boy.

Oliver nodded. 'I do indeed!'

'I know a nice old gent in London who'll give you a bed for nothing – he knows me very well!' The boy sounded very confident.

This offer of a place to sleep, and a free place at that, was extremely tempting, and Oliver accepted gratefully.

'What's your name?' the boy wanted to know.

Oliver told him.

'Mine's Jack Dawkins – they call me the Artful Dodger!' the boy said proudly.

Oliver was none too sure that someone with a name like that was an honest person, but he was so grateful for the Dodger's help that he said nothing.

CHAPTER THREE

Fagin's Gang

WHAT OLIVER TWIST did not know yet was that the Dodger belonged to a gang of pickpockets and robbers. Nor did he know that the Dodger's 'old gent', whose name was Fagin, was the ringleader of the gang.

Fagin's house was in a very old part of London, and Oliver and the Artful Dodger had to walk through a maze of dark,

smelly streets to reach it. Oliver found
that frightening enough, but he was even
more scared when he met Fagin. Fagin
was a very old, shrivelled-up creature with
a villainous-looking face and a mass of
matted red hair.

'Come in, come in, my boy!' Fagin
welcomed Oliver when the Dodger
introduced him. 'We're very glad to
see you!'

Something about Fagin's voice made
Oliver feel cold all over, but the old man
seemed kind enough. He gave Oliver a
meal, then showed him to an old mattress
where he could sleep.

In the days that followed, the Dodger
and other young boys in Fagin's gang
went out picking pockets. They brought
back many handkerchiefs, pocket books
and other objects, which Oliver was given
to sort out. Oliver never suspected that
these things were stolen until one day

when he was allowed to go out with
the Dodger and another boy called
Charley Bates.

The boys seemed to wander aimlessly
through the streets for a long time until,
suddenly, the Dodger halted in a narrow
passageway and drew his companions
back against the wall.

'See that old fellow by the bookstall?'
he whispered, pointing to a prosperous-
looking gentleman on the other side of the
passageway. 'He'll do for us.'

'Very nicely!' agreed Charley Bates.

Charley and the Dodger slipped
across to where the old gentleman stood
reading a book he had picked up. As
Oliver watched in growing alarm, the
Artful Dodger plunged his hand into the
man's pocket, drew out a handkerchief
and handed it to Charley. Then the two
of them ran at full speed round the corner
and out of sight.

Oliver felt a tingle of terror at what he had seen. It was out-and-out stealing, and he was involved! He began to run away, but it was too late. The old gentleman, whose name was Mr Brownlow, had discovered that his expensive handkerchief was missing. 'Stop! Stop, thief!' he shouted. He set off after the fleeing Oliver, and was joined by a growing crowd of people.

A big, rough-looking man soon overtook Oliver and gave him a hefty blow with his fist. Oliver fell sprawling in the mud.

CHAPTER FOUR

New Friends

SOMEONE CALLED A policeman;
Oliver was bundled off to the nearest
police station, and Mr Brownlow followed.
Curiously, he seemed to regret the whole
business, and said so when Oliver was
taken before the magistrate, Mr Fang.

'This boy is not a thief, sir. I am sure of
it!' Mr Brownlow protested. 'Please deal
kindly with him. Besides, I believe he is ill.'

Oliver did indeed look very unwell. All of a sudden, he fell to the floor in a faint.

Just then, an elderly man came rushing into the courtroom. 'Stop! Stop!' he cried.

'Who are you?' Mr Fang demanded crossly.

'I keep the bookstall in the passageway,' the newcomer explained. 'The robbery was committed by another boy, not this poor young fellow!' He pointed to Oliver, still unconscious on the floor.

Mr Fang frowned, and started grumbling about people wasting his time. He could do nothing except dismiss the charge against Oliver.

Oliver was thrown on to the pavement outside the courtroom, where he was soon found by Mr Brownlow.

'Dear me, how pale he is! And he's shivering! He has a fever, I'll be bound!' Mr Brownlow bent down beside Oliver, regarding him anxiously. 'Call a coach, somebody, directly!'

The next thing Oliver knew was that he was in bed in a quiet, shady room. 'What place is this?' he murmured.

A plump, motherly looking old lady appeared beside the bed. There was a sweet, loving expression on her face.

'Hush, dear!' she said softly. 'You must stay quiet now, or you will be ill again!'

The lady's name was Mrs Bedwin, and she was Mr Brownlow's housekeeper. For several more days, she looked after Oliver and saw to his every need, until at last he was well enough to be visited by Mr Brownlow.

'And how do you feel now, dear boy?' the old gentleman wanted to know.

'Oh, much better, sir, and very happy – very grateful indeed for all your goodness to me!'

As Oliver spoke, Mr Brownlow kept staring at him. This poor, neglected waif reminded him of someone, but whom? Then the answer came to him. Of course – the portrait! Mr Brownlow looked up at the picture hanging on the wall just above Oliver's head. It showed a pretty young lady. Mr Brownlow glanced at Oliver and gave a start.

'Mrs Bedwin!' he gasped. 'Don't you see? This boy – his eyes, his mouth, his expression – his whole face is the same as the face in the picture!'

CHAPTER FIVE

He Must Be Found

MEANWHILE, THE ARTFUL Dodger
and Charley were in big trouble with
Fagin for 'losing' Oliver in the street.

When they returned without him,
Fagin flew into a rage and threatened to
throttle both of them. Oliver now knew
quite a lot about the gang and how they
worked, so Fagin was worried in case the
boy had 'peached' – that is, betrayed the

gang to the police.

'He must be found, he must!' Fagin stormed.

'But – but how?' Charley Bates stuttered. 'London's an enormous place, Fagin. Where do we start?'

Fagin's fury suddenly faded away. A cunning gleam came into his eyes. 'Leave that to me, my boy,' he told Charley as he paced the room. 'I'll think of something!'

Fagin did not take long to come up with a plan. One of the thieves in the gang was a girl called Nancy. Fagin told her to go to the police station to see what she could find out about where Oliver was.

At first Nancy refused, for she was afraid of the police. She was more afraid, though, of Bill Sikes, another member of Fagin's gang and a cruel bully of a man.

'Say no, would you?' Bill glowered at Nancy, raising his hand. 'You'll get my fist

in your face!' he threatened. It would not
have been the first time Bill had beaten
Nancy. 'All right, all right,' she said hastily.
'I'll go!'

If she had to run this errand, Nancy
thought, she might as well make a good
job of it. Nancy was a good actress, and
when she got to the police station she
burst into tears. Through her wails and
sobs, she told the policeman that she had
lost her dear little brother. She was lying
and meant Oliver, of course.

'Where is he, oh, where is he?' Nancy
wept. 'I must find him, I must!'

The policeman was a soft-hearted man,
and he was totally deceived by Nancy's
pretence. So he told her that the boy had
been taken away by an old gentleman
who lived somewhere near Pentonville in
north London.

When Nancy returned with this news,
Fagin immediately sent her out again,

together with the Artful Dodger and Charley Bates, to search for the house in Pentonville.

'Oliver has not betrayed us yet!' Fagin muttered nervously. 'Nancy would've learned at the station had he done that! But he must be found before he can talk, or we are all lost!'

CHAPTER SIX

Trapped

OLIVER WAS GOING to fall into
Fagin's hands much more easily than
anyone thought. As he slowly recovered his
health, he tried to think of some way to
repay all the loving care he had received
in Mr Brownlow's house. His chance came
one day when a messenger delivered a
parcel of books for Mr Brownlow, but
left before he could be given some other

volumes which Mr Brownlow had wanted to return to the shop.

'Please let me take them, sir!' Oliver begged. 'I won't be ten minutes! I'll run all the way!'

Oliver's eyes sparkled with eagerness as Mr Brownlow gave him the books and a five-pound note to cover the bill at the bookshop. Oliver set off briskly. He felt very smart in the new set of clothes Mr Brownlow had bought for him. They were the first new clothes Oliver had ever worn, for in the workhouse he wore only ragged old clothes other people had discarded.

He had nearly reached the bookshop when all of a sudden a young woman stepped into his path. She flung her arms round his neck, and to his amazement she started crying: 'Oh, my gracious! I've found him! My dear, lost little brother! I've found him!'

It was Nancy. She had just come out of

a public house, where Fagin and Bill Sikes had been drinking and talking together. She was holding Oliver very tightly as he struggled hard, trying to escape. 'You're not my sister! You're not! I haven't got a sister!' Oliver kept yelling.

Just then, he felt Mr Brownlow's books being snatched from him, and a heavy blow landed on the back of his head. Bill Sikes, hearing the noise and shouting, had come out of the public house to see Oliver struggling with Nancy.

Bill hit Oliver again, then grabbed his collar and began dragging the dazed boy through a maze of narrow, winding streets to the place where Oliver dreaded even more than the terrible workhouse – Fagin's den.

'Delighted to see you looking so well, my boy!' Fagin said in a menacing voice that made Oliver shiver right down his spine. He was trapped!

Oliver's heart sank when he thought of his new, kind friends at Mr Brownlow's house. What would they think when he did not return? Perhaps they would think he had run away with Mr Brownlow's five pounds and the valuable books, to say nothing of his fine, new suit of clothes.

'If they thought that, I could not bear it!' Oliver said to himself, feeling distraught.

CHAPTER SEVEN

Threatening Words

DURING THE NEXT few days, Fagin made certain that Oliver had no chance to escape.

All the while, Mr Brownlow was frantically searching for Oliver. He sent out servants to scour the streets for the boy, and asked everyone he met if they had spotted him. He even put an advertisement in the newspaper, offering a reward for information about Oliver. But all his efforts achieved nothing. As far as Mr Brownlow knew, the boy had vanished.

In the meantime, Fagin was trying to train Oliver to be a criminal. He told him how exciting it was to go out thieving, and what a fortune he could make. Oliver did not believe him.

One day, Fagin told Oliver, 'I'm sending you over to Bill Sikes, my boy! We've a nice little job for you!'

Nancy came to collect Oliver. She seemed very upset, and with good reason, too.

Despite her rough ways and sharp tongue, she had a kind heart. She had become very fond of Oliver, and she knew that he was in great danger now. Fagin and Bill Sikes planned to use him to help them in a big robbery.

When they reached Bill's house, Bill

took Oliver to one side. 'Do you know what this is?' he asked, showing Oliver a small pistol.

Oliver gulped and nodded. Bill picked up the pistol, loaded it with bullets and then placed the barrel against Oliver's head. It felt cold and hard.

'We're going out, you and me,' Sikes growled. 'And if you speak a word to anyone I'll blow your head off!' It was not a threat Oliver could easily forget.

CHAPTER EIGHT

The Burglary

BILL SIKES TOOK Oliver to a dank, dilapidated house well outside London. There, Sikes's two accomplices were waiting. After gathering up their pistols, crowbars and other equipment, they all set off into the pitch-black, foggy night.

Oliver now realized the frightful crime in which he was involved, and begged Bill Sikes to let him go. 'I'll never come near

London again, I promise!' Oliver cried.
'Please, Mr Sikes, please!'

But Bill had a job for Oliver to do, and
he meant to make sure he did it. When
they reached the house where the robbery
was going to take place, Bill forced open
a tiny window with his crowbar. 'Get in
there!' he told Oliver in a husky voice.
'Then open the front door and let us in.
I'll point this pistol at you all the way,
so don't try any tricks – or I'll shoot
you dead!'

Despite this threat, Oliver decided to
try and warn the people in the house.
Once inside, he started running upstairs
to the family's rooms.

'Come back, you wretch!' cried Bill
Sikes.

All at once, two men appeared at the
top of the stairs. One of them held a
lantern, the other a pistol. Oliver heard
him fire it, and felt a fierce, hot pain in his

arm. Then there was a crash, another shot and the sound of a bell. Oliver felt himself being lifted up and dragged outside.

The burglary had gone wrong. The two men in the house had raised the alarm, and Bill Sikes and his gang could only run, taking Oliver too.

Oliver was hardly aware of what was going on. He was dazed, and his arm hurt dreadfully. Blackness closed in on him, and he fainted.

CHAPTER NINE

Kindness – and a Disappointment

WHEN OLIVER AWOKE, it was morning, and he was lying in a ditch, where Bill Sikes had left him. Bill and the other robbers were nowhere to be seen, for they had all managed to escape and had hurried back to London.

Oliver felt weak, and the shawl Bill had tied round his arm was soaked with blood. With a tremendous effort, he struggled to his feet and staggered along until he reached a road. A short way on, he came to a house. With a flicker of fear, he realized that it was the very house where the robbery had been attempted the previous night.

Oliver wanted to run away, but his strength failed him.

Inside, the servants heard a noise. When they opened the front door, one of them, Mr Giles, recognized Oliver.

'Here's the thief! I shot him!' he shouted.

'Giles!' a soft voice whispered from the top of the stairs. 'Hush, or you'll frighten my aunt!'

It was a young girl, very slender and sweet-faced, with kind, deep blue eyes. She came quietly down the stairs and looked at Oliver, who had been carried inside and was lying on the hall floor.

'Oh, the poor little fellow!' the girl exclaimed. 'Carry him upstairs, Giles.

Gently now, be careful!'

The young lady, whose name was Rose, ordered the doctor to be brought.

The bullet, the doctor discovered, had broken Oliver's arm. The injury was not serious, but it would be a long time before the arm mended and Oliver felt well again.

Rose, her aunt Mrs Maylie, the doctor, whose name was Losberne, and all the servants – even Giles – were very kind and gentle towards Oliver.

Oliver was very grateful for his good fortune, but, all the same, he wanted more than anything to return to London and find Mr Brownlow.

Dr Losberne offered to take Oliver to London in his carriage. When they reached the street where Mr Brownlow lived, Oliver spotted the house at once. 'That one! There! The white house!' he cried, pointing excitedly.

But Oliver's excitement soon faded, for the house was all shut up and there was a notice outside saying 'To Let'. Dr Losberne sent his coachman next door to make enquiries, and he returned with the sad news that Mr Brownlow had gone away six weeks previously, far across the Atlantic Ocean to the West Indies.

Oliver burst into tears. It was all too terrible! Mr Brownlow must have left thinking Oliver was a deceitful, dishonest little wretch. Now he would never learn the truth.

Chapter Ten

A Curious Tale

DR LOSBERNE TOOK Oliver back to his friends in the country, and for a long time the boy was very sad. Oliver could not believe there would be a happy ending to his search – but there was.

Three months later, Dr Losberne took Oliver to London again, and Rose Maylie came with them. They were all delighted to discover that Mr Brownlow had

returned and was very anxious for news of
Oliver. The old gentleman greeted Oliver
warmly and Mrs Bedwin, the housekeeper,
hugged him and kissed him joyfully.

When all the greetings were over,
and Oliver was well occupied telling
Mrs Bedwin of his adventures, Rose asked
Mr Brownlow if she could see him alone,
for she had a secret to confide.

Mr Brownlow took Rose to a quiet
room, where she told him a very curious
tale.

A day or two before, a wretched young
girl called Nancy had come to see Rose
at her hotel in London. Nancy told Rose
about a man called Monks, who had
come to Fagin's house a few days earlier,
while Nancy was there.

Fagin and Monks knew each other
already, for they had planned the burglary
at the house where Rose lived with Mrs
Maylie. Fagin took Monks off to another

room and Nancy, listening at the door, overheard them talking of Oliver. Monks said that Oliver was his younger brother, and he wanted Fagin to arrange to have him killed so that he could get his hands on the boy's fortune.

'I heard Monks mention your name, Miss,' Nancy had explained to Rose, 'and where you were staying in London. That's how I knew where to find you.' Then Nancy began to cry bitterly. 'Please, Miss, don't let darling Oliver come to any harm! I'd give my own life to save him. Honest I would!'

'But what can I do?' Rose had protested. 'How can I find this dreadful Mr Monks?'

'I can help you,' Nancy promised. 'If you'll find a gentleman to help and protect you, I'll tell you where Monks can be found.'

'Where shall we meet you?' asked Rose.

'On London Bridge. I'll be there every Sunday night, between eleven and midnight,' Nancy said.

Mr Brownlow was astonished and intrigued by Rose's story. 'There's a mystery here, right enough,' he said. 'Nancy is taking a great risk for Oliver's sake. She's a very brave soul,' he muttered. 'The thieves and criminals who are her companions will surely kill her if they discover what she has done. Still,' he went on, 'we cannot let this chance slip by. Oliver's fortune, and his life, are at stake. We must meet this girl and learn all we can from her!'

CHAPTER ELEVEN

The Meeting

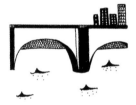

NANCY WAS NOT on London Bridge
the first Sunday night, for Bill Sikes, who
was in a very bad mood, threatened to
beat her if she left the house.

Fagin was there at the time, and he
thought there was something very odd
about Nancy's manner and behaviour.
Why did she so want to go out? He
decided to send one of his boys to follow

Nancy on the next Sunday night, to see where she went and whom she met.

The spy faithfully carried out Fagin's instructions. He watched as Nancy met Rose and Mr Brownlow on the bridge just after midnight. Unseen and unheard, the boy crept close and heard Nancy describe the tall, lean Mr Monks, the public house he often visited, and at what times.

'You can recognize him easily,' Nancy said. 'There is a mark on his throat, a big red…'

'A red mark!' Mr Brownlow interrupted her. 'A mark like a burn or a scald?'

Rose and Nancy exchanged surprised looks.

'Why, yes!' Nancy replied. 'Do you know him?'

Mr Brownlow nodded, a grim expression on his face. 'Yes, yes, I think I do!' he muttered.

Mr Brownlow lost no time. The very

next day, he went out with two of his manservants to look for Monks. Quite near the public house of which Nancy had spoken, they spotted their prey.

Before Monks knew what was happening, the manservants grabbed him, bundled him into a hackney carriage and drove off at a smart pace to Mr Brownlow's house.

CHAPTER TWELVE

The Mystery
Is Solved

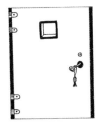

MONKS WAS LED to a back room.

'Go outside and lock the door!'
Mr Brownlow told the manservants.
'Mr Monks and I will speak together
alone!' The servants looked doubtful, for
Monks seemed dangerous. Nevertheless,
they obeyed.

When they had gone, Mr Brownlow
looked at Monks sadly for a few moments.

'I thought this was the man,' Mr Brownlow reflected silently. 'He's the son of my best friend. Nancy described him well.' Aloud he said, 'Your name is not Monks, it's Edward Leeford!'

Monks gave a start of surprise. 'How d'you know that?' he growled suspiciously.

Mr Brownlow sighed. 'Because I knew your father, Edwin Leeford, and his sister, who died many, many years ago — on the very day she and I were to be married!'

A flicker of pain crossed Mr Brownlow's face as he remembered his young bride-to-be. 'I know that your father and mother were unhappy together, and that they parted when you were still a boy. And…' Mr Brownlow paused for a second. 'I know that you have a brother!'

Monks's eyes narrowed. 'I have no brother. I was an only child!'

'The only child of your father's marriage, yes!' said Mr Brownlow. 'But

after your parents parted, your father fell
in love with a beautiful young girl called
Agnes Fleming. Poor Agnes died giving
birth to their child — a boy who, by the
grace of God, later fell into my hands!
I knew what Agnes looked like, you see,
for your father gave me her portrait, and
the boy looked exactly like her!'

Monks was utterly dumbfounded
by these revelations. However, the old
gentleman had not yet finished. He told
how Oliver had disappeared on the way
to the bookshop, and how he had searched
for him.

'I knew you could solve this mystery
for me,' Mr Brownlow told Monks. 'I
also knew of your criminal life and that
you had escaped to the West Indies. So I
followed you there!'

The voyage to the West Indies had been
fruitless. By the time Mr Brownlow had
arrived there, Monks had already returned

to England. Mr Brownlow made the long journey home again, and scoured the streets seeking Monks for many weeks. But not until he heard Nancy speak of the man with the scar did the old gentleman have any clue to where Monks was.

'You were a wretched child, and you are still a scoundrel and robber!' Mr Brownlow declared. 'You plan to have young Oliver murdered, don't you, so you can have all your father's money!'

'You can't prove anything against me!' Monks blustered, turning very pale.

'Oh, but I can!' Mr Brownlow retorted. 'I know about Fagin and the plot you hatched together!'

'F-Fagin?' Monks stammered. 'Who is he?'

'Shall we call the police, then, and let you deny it to them?'

Monks looked terrified. 'No, no, don't!' he pleaded. 'They – they will hang me!'

Mr Brownlow gave a sigh of satisfaction. 'Ah, then you will surely do as I demand!' he cried. 'You must sign a document giving Oliver his rightful share of your father's money!'

Monks looked miserable. He thought of the police cell, the courtroom and the hangman's rope that would surely be round his neck if he refused.

'Very well,' he muttered. 'Oliver shall have his inheritance – I promise!'

CHAPTER THIRTEEN

A Bright Future

POOR NANCY, WHOSE love for Oliver
made her take such great risks on his
behalf, would have been very happy to
know of the boy's good fortune. But,
sadly, Nancy had paid a high price for
her actions. When Fagin's spy told him
about Nancy's meeting with Rose and
Mr Brownlow on London Bridge, Fagin
had been enraged. He sent for Bill Sikes

and told him the story. Bill, always a brutal man, took his pistol and cold-heartedly shot Nancy dead.

Even as Mr Brownlow and Monks were talking, the police were out hunting for the murderer. That very night, they cornered Bill Sikes in his hiding place.

In a panic, Bill clambered out on to the roof, taking with him a rope to let himself down to the ground and make his escape. But he missed his footing and, as he fell, the rope tangled round his neck. The rope tightened, and Bill choked to death.

That same day, acting on information given to them by Mr Brownlow, the police arrested Fagin, together with several of his boys. At his trial, Fagin was condemned to end his life on the gallows.

As for Oliver Twist, Mr Brownlow adopted him as his own son. He took him to live in the country, with Mrs Bedwin. Oliver was very happy there, for he loved

the fresh, green countryside with its beautiful fields and flowers and trees.

Once, Oliver had been a poor, misused orphan boy whose only home was the workhouse. Now, his future was bright and life offered him much happiness. He had the inheritance his father had intended for him. Above all, now that Fagin was dead and his gang of thieves and killers broken up, Oliver need never be afraid of them again.

Collect more fantastic

LADYBIRD CLASSICS

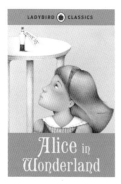

Alice in Wonderland

9781409311232

Oliver Twist

9781409311256

Treasure Island

9781409311287

BLACK BEAUTY

9781409311249

GULLIVER'S Travels

9781409311270

The Secret Garden

9781409311263